Acoustic Rooster's

Barnyard Boogie

Starring **Indigo Blume**

Kwame Alexander

Illustrated by

Tim Bowers

PUBLISHED BY SLEEPING BEAR PRESS™

Today was a good day.

We laughed and danced while cleaning up for the Garden City Community Festival.

The people were happy.

My city is my city, and my responsibility.
If you see a soda can, pick it up. If you see a plastic bag, pick it up.
If you see a newspaper, pick it up.

But then everything changed in a flash
when Elijah said:

"Hey, Indigo, the whole school is coming to
watch you sing at the festival tomorrow!"

Mr. Woody chimed in, "There are posters all
over the city, and the city next to us, and the
city next to that city too."

"There'll be hundreds of families there,"
said Samantha.

Singing in front of HUNDREDS of people?
Not Me.
I. AM. NOT. SINGING.

I may be from Garden City,
but I took a ride to PANIC CITY
and ran straight home.

You're the bravest songbird I know.

My mom says
I have a voice full of
sunshine and wonder.

I do love to sing.
    But in front of
THOUSANDS of people?

NOOOOOO
    WAY!

Dad says he believes in me too.
And that I should believe in me.

Be brave. Be a star. Believe.

I want to be brave.
I want to be courageous.

But how?

How am I supposed to sing at the Garden City Community Festival in front of **MILLIONS** of people tomorrow?

I'm better with just me. In front of an audience I totally freeze.

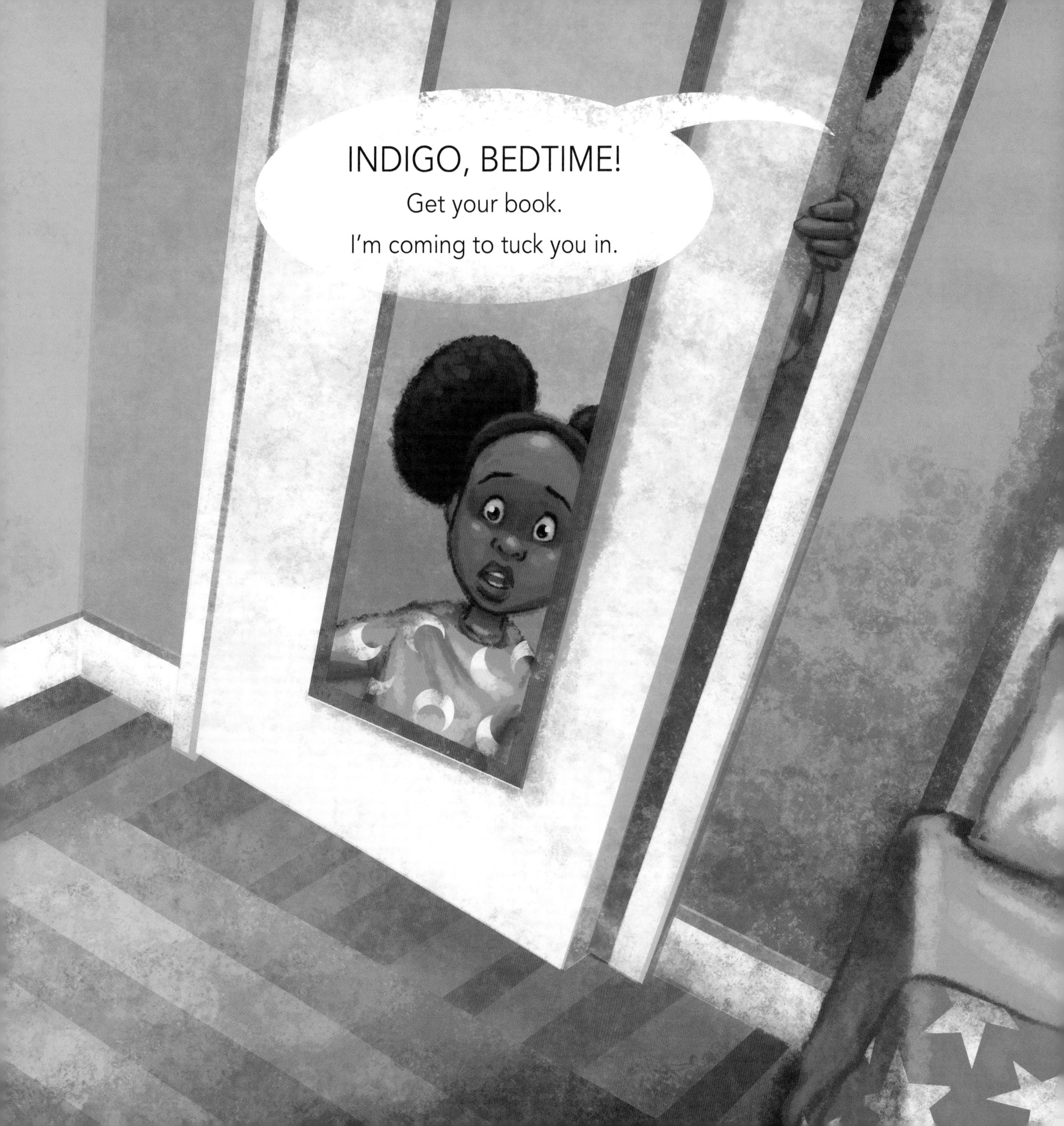
INDIGO, BEDTIME!
Get your book.
I'm coming to tuck you in.

The last thing I remember is falling asleep to Mom's singing,
the night wind blowing through my window . . .

and waking up—GET THIS—inside a barn
full of very familiar animals
flapping and waddling on stage.

I recognized Acoustic Rooster
from my favorite book.
So I figured it had to be a dream. . . .

"Wait, who's that? When did you blow in?"
Miss Dairy Parton asked, looking down at me.

"This is a closed rehearsal," said Chickee Minaj.

"I didn't blow in. And I beg your pardon," I said.
"I'm Indigo Blume from Garden City. I know you guys!
You're the Barnyard Band, right?"

"We are indeed. You name it, we play it—
jazz, rock, country, gospel, go-go, and hip hop,"
said Acoustic Rooster. "Why don't you join us?"

And just as he handed me a tambourine . . .

the wind started . . .

blowing hard . . .

and roaring loud. . . .

It sounded like . . .

a train in the sky . . .

a HURRITRAIN!

Everything was flying **everywhichaway.**

Half the barn was SMASHED
and SHATTERED to pieces.

The band mooed
and moaned,
quacked
and groaned.

Then an idea came to me. . . .

Let's work together to clean this up. If you see something out of place, pick it up. Follow me!

We moved all the rocks,

rocked the rakes,
then raked up all the leaves.

Before we knew it, the barnyard
started looking better.
Our clean-up plan was working wonderfully.

The animals were happy.

Until . . .

"This is bad and that ain't good," sang Miss Dairy Parton.

"All that work for nothing," hollered Chickee Minaj.

"We have no home," said Duck Ellington.

"And now we'll forever roam," wailed Mules Davis.

"Maybe we can raise money
to rebuild the barn," said Rooster.
"We can tour, play music for money,
at schools, libraries—"

"Or we can play right here. . . .
LET'S THROW A BENEFIT CONCERT!" I screamed.

"A barnyard benefit to save the barn! Come on, that's crazy . . .
enough . . .
to just . . .
maybe . . .
work," said Acoustic Rooster.

"We'll call it the Barnyard Boogie," I said.
"Let's do this, friends!"

I volunteered to be
the backstage manager
for the Barnyard Boogie.

Everyone warmed up
and we were ready to go.
Or so we thought. . . .

The music was hoppin' and poppin'.
My friends performed
like the barnyard was the Apollo Theater—
or the Kennedy Center.

"I've got some baaaaaddddd news," said Acoustic Rooster.

"Miss Dairy Parton has lost her voice!" he continued.

"Say it isn't so!" Duck Ellington quacked.

Oh no, the diva is hoarse . . . even though she is a cow!
Oh no, the diva is hoarse! Who's going to sing the finale now?

"We need you to sing, Indigo," said Rooster.

"I am no star, like Miss Dairy Parton," I squeaked.

"But you are INDIGO! Believe in yourself,"
Rooster replied.

I want to be brave. I want to be courageous.
I'm just scared to sing in front of a crowd.

Be a star
in your mind.
Just open your mouth
and let it shine.

I stood on the stage.
The spotlight was bright.
I opened my mouth . . .

and my voice broke free.
It soared like a sparrow,
and I sang.
The crowd went bananas.
Even the clouds clapped.

With a little help from so many friends, we raised enough money to start rebuilding the barn.

Oh yes, we don't have to leave the farm. Now we can stay and rebuild the barn!

We hugged and danced and celebrated till it was way past my bedtime.

When I woke up,
I was back in my bedroom.

Ready to be brave.
Ready to be courageous
Ready to . . .

SING at the festival tonight.
Ready to shine like a bright star.

Sometimes dreams can feel so real. . . .

By the way, I rocked the
Garden City Community Festival,
and everyone was happy.

Especially me.

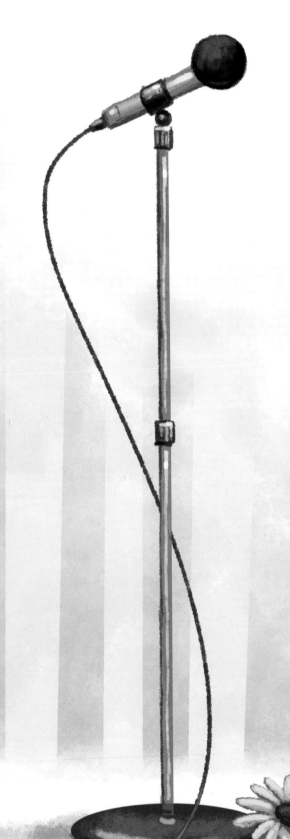

Dedicated to Mary and Randy, my partners-in-rhyme
—Kwame

To Brylie, Grady, and Caleb
—TB

Text Copyright © 2020 Kwame Alexander
Illustration Copyright © 2020 Tim Bowers
Design © 2020 Sleeping Bear Press

SLEEPING BEAR PRESS™

2395 South Huron Parkway, Suite 200,
Ann Arbor, MI 48104
www.sleepingbearpress.com
© Sleeping Bear Press

Printed and bound in the United States.
10 9 8 7 6 5 4 3 2

Library of Congress Cataloging-in-Publication Data
Names: Alexander, Kwame, author. | Bowers, Tim, illustrator.
Title: Acoustic Rooster's Barnyard Boogie starring Indigo Blume / Kwame Alexander ; illustrated by Tim Bowers.
Description: Ann Arbor, MI : Sleeping Bear Press, [2020] | Audience: Ages 6-10. | Summary: Afraid of singing in front of a large crowd, Indigo
dreams about Acoustic Rooster and his band and, after a storm flattens their barn, helps organize a concert fundraiser to rebuild it.
Identifiers: LCCN 2020033044 | ISBN 9781534111141 (hardcover) | ISBN 9781534111349 (paperback)
Subjects: CYAC: Stage fright—Fiction. | Singing—Fiction. | Concerts—Fiction. | Musicians—Fiction. | Domestic animals—Fiction.
Classification: LCC PZ7.A37723 Aco 2020 | DDC [E]—dc23 LC record available at https://lccn.loc.gov/2020033044